JAMES KOCHALKA

THE GLORKIAN WARRIOR AND THE MUSTACHE OF DESTINY

:01
First Second
New York

for Eli and Oliver

VISIT GLORKIANWARRIOR.COM

Published by First Second

First Second is an imprint of Roaring Brook Press, a division of Holtzbrinck Publishing Holdings Limited Partnership
175 Fifth Avenue, New York, New York 10010

"Glorkian Warrior" first appeared in *Popgun* Volume 2

Cataloging-in-Publication Data is on file at the Library of Congress.

Paperback ISBN 978-1-62672-022-0
Hardcover ISBN 978-1-62672-372-6

First edition 2016
Book design by Danielle Ceccolini

Printed in China by Macmillan Production (Asia) Ltd., Kowloon Bay, Hong Kong (supplier code 10)

Paperback: 10 9 8 7 6 5 4 3 2 1
Hardcover: 10 9 8 7 6 5 4 3 2 1

Drawn with Kimberly 6H pencil and Windsor & Newton size 1 brush with Windsor & Newton Black Indian Ink on smooth 2-ply Strathmore Bristol paper, colored in Photoshop on an Apple iMac with a Wacom Cintiq.

Layout in InDesign, hand lettered.

CHAPTER ZERO

CHUMF CHUMF
VVVVVVV
ARg! Cut it out, Super Backpack!
That's TOO BRIGHT.

A GIANT flying mustache!
Scary!

RUN, BOSS! RUN!
I'm RUNNING!

I don't WANT to grow a GIANT MUSTACHE!
I'm... I'm...
Hey!
I CAN'T RUN.

There are CHILDREN ON YOUR LEG!
AAH! Children?!
That's DISGUSTING!
They're like WARTS.

Get off! Get off!
shake shake
shake

Boss, what is that on your head?
Something is on my head?

FLAP
FLAP
Waa ha ha HA! Help me, Super Backpack! HELP! Ha ha ha!
Ha ha HA ha!
The whole world is BONKERS, and I can't stop laughing!
Ha HA!

Oh.

It was a DREAM.

Zzz
Little Gonk is still asleep. I better be quiet.

I'll just tiptoe downstairs and get Super Backpack...
And some HOT COFFEE.

And just forget that CRAZY DREAM ever happened.
Z
tip toe tip toe

Actually... GONK am secretly AWAKE!

Pssst! Hey, Guys! It am me, GONK.
Am you READY?

CHAPTER ONE

Good morning, Glorkian Warrior!

And good morning to you too, Little Cup of Coffee!

Ooh! Ooh! I just had a BRILLIANT IDEA!
DING!
What is it, Boss?

I think I just invented TALKING COFFEE!
I'm a GENIUS!
No, Boss. No you DIDN'T!

Coffee can't TALK.
People used to say the same thing about BACKPACKS.
Listen... "Good morning, Coffee!"

tink
Shhh.

Right there! Did you hear that?
TALKING COFFEE!

And delicious too.
SSSIP

BLARG!

BAM!
Ooof!
JUMP
Hi-YA!

How was that?
GONK SNUCK UP!
AND then Hi-YA!

Was that GOOD like a REAL Glorkian Warrior?
No, Gonk. You SCARED my coffee.
SSIP

Aw. Hear that?
thump thump thump
Its little heart is THUMPING. I better take another sip to calm it down.
Boss, that's not-
BLARGS!
thump!
LEAP
BAM!
Gweep!
How's thats?

Coffee, stop JUMPING!
CALM down and let me dRINK YOU.
Here's MINE!
Ow!
KICK
BRONK!
BLAMMO
WOWS!
Cool!

Ha ha!
We all gots you!
Was that pretty good?
Huff, huff, GRONK!
Pretty good? This coffee is AMAZING. It really wakes you UP.

Me am Gonk. Me LIVE here, remember?
I'm Doonky!
Doonkies are here because-
BRONK is BRONK!

Wow!
He has real-life official Glorkian Warrior boots!

Can I have them?
What? NO!

PEAS can I?
Can Gonk try grown-up coffee?
Can Doonkies try blasting stuffs with your Super Backpacks?
NO!
BRONK CAN BRONK?

Can GONK do this?
Can DOONKIES do THATS?
May CRAZY FACE?
CANS BRONK BRONK BRONK?

No!
NO!
NO!
NO.
PEAS?!

NO to EVERYONE and EVERYTHING!
Even PEAS!

Uh-oh. Him MAD NOW.
Whoops.
We better get SERIOUS.

Junior-Junior Glorkian Warriors reporting for duty, Sir!
BRONK!

CHAPTER TWO

Well, t

I guess.

See ya later, kids.

Good-bye.

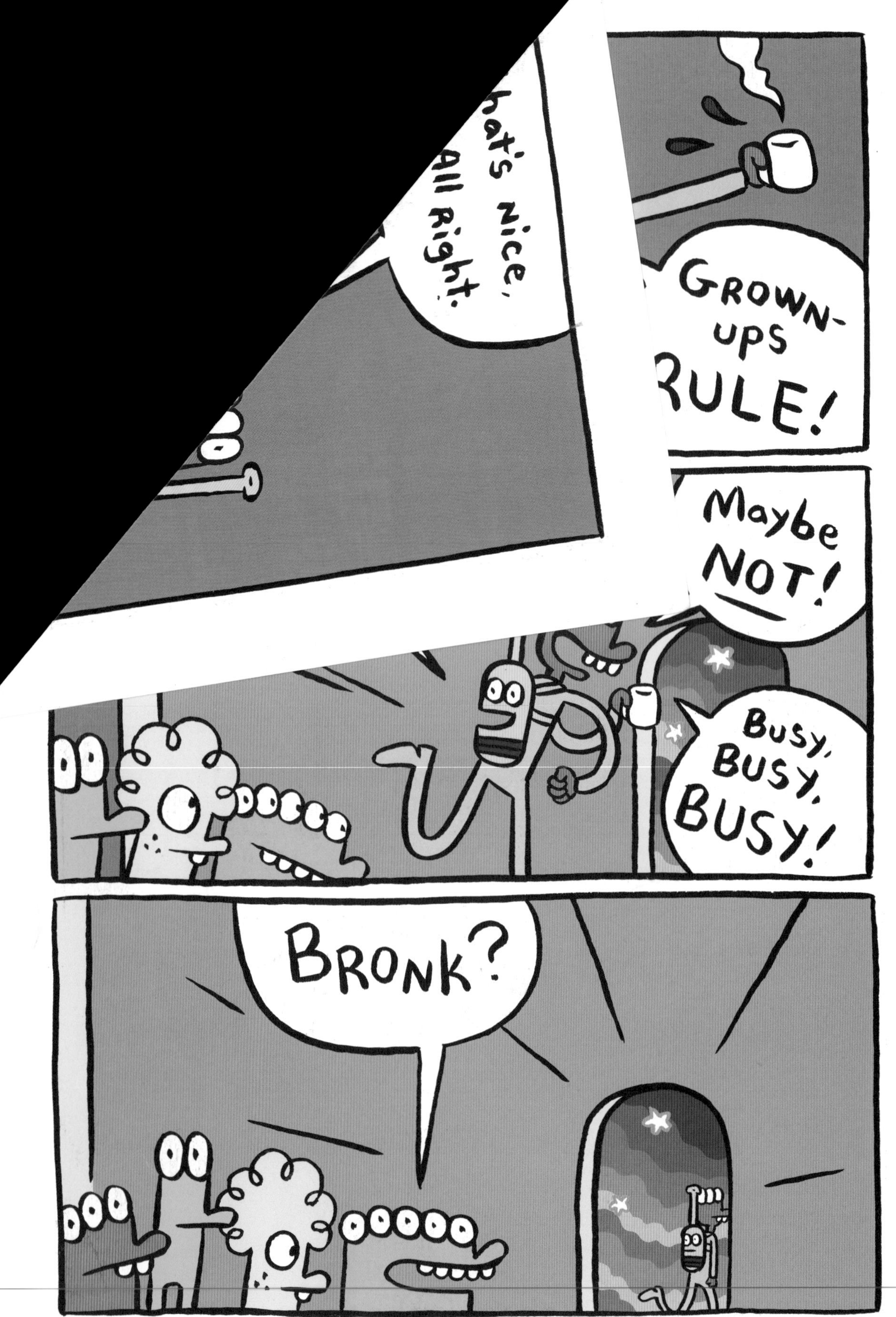
hat's nice,
All right.
GROWN-UPS
RULE!
Maybe NOT!
Busy, BUSY, BUSY!
BRONK?

Now off we go on GLORK PATROL.
Just ME and my best friend.
And NO pesky kids.

You're my best friend too, Boss. I Really like going on patrol with you.
Huh?

Me and you!
No, I mean my new talking-coffee friend.

Boss!
Talking Coffee isn't REAL!
Now, now, Super Backpack.
Don't be silly.

If my coffee friend wasn't REAL could I do this?
SSSip

It's real coffee, but it's not a real person.

If it's not a real person then how come his name is Charlie?
ANSWER me that.
His name is NOT CHARLIE!

Fred?
Bucky?
No!
Thomas?
No!
No!

None of those names? Well, then maybe my coffee is a GIRL.

HER NAME IS WENDY.
Hello, WENDY!

What, you got a problem now with GIRLS, Super Backpack?
Girls are people TOO, you know.

JUST TURN AROUND.
AROUND WHAT?

It looks like our Glork Patrol has turned into a Glork PARADE.
Oh!
Patrol, patrol.
Patrols.
Patrol patrol patrol.
BRONK!

CHAPTER THREE

Ridiculous children!
I already said goodbye.
Why are you following me?

Boss!
We can't let all those LITTLE KIDS follow us on Glork Patrol.
Someone could get HURT.

That's right, kids. One of you might hurt me.
Also, only REAL Glorkian Warriors can go on Glork Patrol.
And only their Super Backpacks can go too.
Sorry. Too bad.

Yeah, that's AWESOME! You can just teach us how to be REAL Glorkian Warriors, the same as YOU are!
Doonkies like to LEARNS.
Ooh! Teach GONK to be a Super Backpack!
Bronk the BRONK to BRONK!
Well, that's an interesting idea.
Yay!
HOORAYS!
Yes!
BRONK!
No, Boss. It isn't.
There are too many of them.

Then just pick ME! I've got the face of a HERO.
Hey!
Right?
Just LOOK at me!

Well, I guess I see some pimples.
Those are my HANDSOME HERO spots.
Look at us!

See? Doonkies are almost Glorkian Warriors already.
See?
Gonk am the Super Backpack!
BRONK!

All Right. I've made my decision. I know which one of you I will take with me to TRAIN.
Me!
Me!
Me!
BRONK!
No, Boss! You CAN'T!
Not even one!

I choose Wendy!
The world's first talking COFFEE!
Hooray!
What? Oh.

CHAPTER FOUR

Oh, what a happy day!
I'll teach you to be the best Glorkian Warrior EVER!
Sorry, kids. The answer is NO.

You told LIES to Doonkies!
You said he would take us on a GLORK PATROL ADVENTURE!
BRONK!

GONK NO lie!
GONK Really went ON a GlORKY venture once.
GONK even "Save the day."

LIES!
The LIES of a LYING LIAR.
Noooo.

Come ON, guys.
DOONKies don't PLAY with you ANYMORES.
NO!
BRONK!

Gonk am SORRY!
Come back!
Don't say NO play with GONK.

Oh, me am sad! Sad and confused.
How come why am this HAPPENING to GONK?
Why?

The whole world am turning upside downy.
Nothing make ANY sense.
Why? Why? Why?

Wait!

Wait wait wait!

That am it! Gonk figured it out!

I guess we'll never be Glorkian Warriors now. Phooey.
Also, Doonkies LIKED playing with Gonks.
Sad Bronk.

Stop!
Gonk says STOP!

Good news!

Gonk know why Glorkian Warrior say "NO!" Gonk know why Glorkian Warrior make Gonk CRY.
Gonk know the secret!

Him say "NO" to make us cry and give up. But it am just a test. A real Glorky Warrior NEVER give up.

We supposed to not give ups too.

Oh yeah! And if you really think about it, he never even really said "NO" exactly.
Yeah it was him's BACKPACKS that said "NO."
BRONK?
Yes!
Come on! Let's show him how the Junior-Junior Glorkian Warriors never give up!
Doonkies are NO ups giving ALL the times!
Junior-Junior BRONK!
Yay!

CHAPTER FIVE

Patrol, patrol, patrol!

This is how you do it, Wendy!

Fine. Step Right in then.

GWEEP!

That...
That's NO HOLE!
That's a... a...
Well, I guess it IS a hole.

But Wendy's not scared, are you, Wendy?
Even though it's only her first day, I think she's READY!
She's ready to PATROL the HOLE!

That's great, Boss. But why are you taking me off now?
Well, if Wendy is going to patrol the hole like a real Glorkian Warrior... she's going to need her own real Super Backpack!
That's YOU!

I'll strap you on like...
BOSS!
I don't get it!

TA-DA!
Boss, what are you doing?

Can you GUESS?
Boss! Don't just DROP us!
Nooooooo!

CHAPTER SIX

Hey!
Wait for Doonkies!
And for Gonk!
BRONK!
Oh my GOSH! It's a stampede!
The children!
Children! Be careful!
YAY!
A JUMPING stampede!
LOOK out!
LEAP

AAAAH!

It's time to get SERIOUS!

Wendy! Save me!

I'm too YOUNG to DIE SERIOUS!
What's happening to Doonkies?
Doonkies are confused.
BRONK!
CANONBALL!
Ha ha! Good idea, GONK.
Watch this.
Bellyflop!
Boss! NO!

WUMP

bounce
Oh!
Oh!
Oh NO!

CLUNK

High Dive Champion of the WORLD!
That's ME.
I. WIN!
My handsome face hurts.
Ows.
BRONK BRONK Ouch.
GONK want a REMATCH.

CHAPTER SEVEN

Wow! Look how far we FELL.

One time Gonk fell in the potty.

Me think maybe BRONK broke him eye.
BRONK eye? BRONK EYE!
Don't WORRY, BRONK. You still have lots of OTHER eyes.
Yay BRONK!
Ha ha!
And there's Wendy!
And she's still got some of the GOOD STUFF in her.
Potato OCTOPUS.
SLOSH

Mmm...
Ssssip

Wait, what did you say?
Broccoli bubblegum.

Super Backpack!
What's WRONG with you?
Potatopus octobubble.

I don't UNDERSTAND you, Super Backpack.
Banana cracker snack-pack chicken licker.
Pitcher plant.

Banana bubble MEMORY GLITCH.
HAPPY BIRTHDAY DAY.

I don't know what you're talking about, Super Backpack!
Stop doing that!
Shake Shake shake
Happy slappy flappy bird.
Stop talking silly baby talk! You're freaking me out.
Wait.
Baby talk?

You think you can understand **this**?

Mountain Britches Flappy Barfday!

Yes.

Maybes.

BRONK.

PROBably FOR SURE.

Banana.
Yellow.
Snack pack.
Back pack!
That mean SUPER BACKPACK!
That am HIM!
Now Doonkies take turns.
Monkey DITCHES!
MEMORY GLITCHES!
HAPPY BIRTHDAY O'CLOCK.
Ooh, ooh!
We need to reset his MEMORY CLOCK to DAY ONE.
BRONK!
Ooh! Ooh!
Bronk know!
Bronk means BRONK!

I think that means Super Backpack is having a memory glitch and we have to reset him back to his factory settings because he BRONKED his head in the fall!
BRONK!
Wow. You kids are like baby-talk GENIUSES.
I'm not just another HANDSOME FACE.
I'm also a SMARTY PANTS.
Except without pants.

CHAPTER EIGHT

Well, anyhoooo...

When I wake up in the morning and need to reset MY memory clock back to the factory settings...

I just drink a cup of HOT WENDY!

Good morning, Boss!

Hahaha! Hello, sleepyhead!

Boss, what just happened?
Oh, you know. Blah, blah, blah, something something.
And we all lived happily ever after!
The end!
Happily ever after?
That's Right!

Happily ever after at the bottom of a GIANT HOLE?
Well... yeah.
Sure looks like it.
BRONK.

CHAPTER NINE

All Right, fine.

If no one wants to live happily ever after at the bottom of a Really cool hole then we can all climb out.

But, Boss!

Come on, everybody.

What?
Are you kidding?

Haven't you ever had an ADVENTURE in a HOLE before?
I have them all the time.

Didn't you guys even read "The Glorkian Warrior Eats Adventure Pie"? You know, my LAST big adventure? They wrote a book about it.
I fall down a hole in that one too.

Oh, fine.
SLIDE

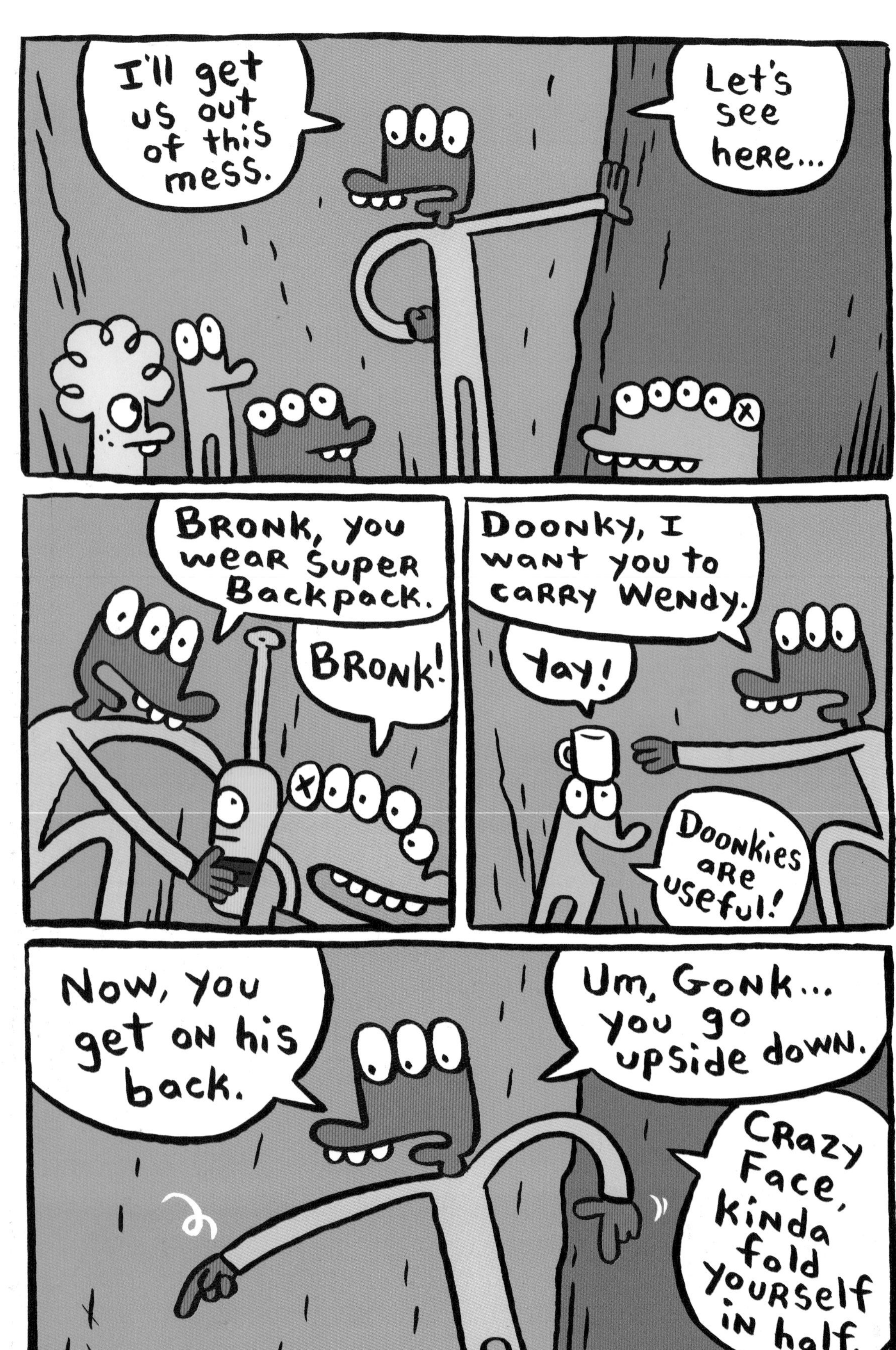
I'll get us out of this mess.
Let's see here...
BRONK, you wear Super Backpack.
BRONK!
Doonky, I want you to carry Wendy.
Yay!
Doonkies are useful!
Now, you get on his back.
Um, Gonk... you go upside down.
Crazy Face, kinda fold yourself in half.

Great!

Doonkies are balancing!

Now, up we go... I guess...
Doonkies can DO it. I believes in Doonkies!

CHAPTER TEN

Doonkies climbed! All the way to the tops!

HOORays!

Good job, Doonky!

Me too!

No, another GIANT HOLE!
Boss! Don't step there!
step!
Whoops. Too late.
Swan dive.
Pencil dives!
Crazyball!
Belly BRONK!

WUMPO SPLAT!
Oooh! This hole is FANCIER than the other one.
It's got special golden stairs!

Whoever made it even built a giant golden statue of me so I'd feel Right at home!

How thoughtful!

Wows!

Weird.

You must be even more famous than I thought you were!
I KNOW!
I KNOW!
I'm so proud of me.
Will they makes a golden statues of DOONKIES someday?
Golden BRONK!
After this adventure they will probably make golden statues of all of us.
AND TEN of me.
Cool.
Yay BRONK!
Happy times!
GOLD am GONK'S New favorite color.
Boss, stop teasing the children.
No one is going to make golden —YURK!
SNATCH

Oh, don't be jealous, Super Backpack.
You're already golden.
Now it's our turn.
Boss!
Sorry, Backpack. It's only fair.
Aaah! Aaah!
No!
Well, there's no need to be a BABY about it.
Don't throw a fit.
Help! Help!
Wait. Who are YOU?
Ha HAHAHA!!
It's the statues guy.

Welcome to the Temple of Quackaboodle!
Super Backpack?!
I'm Quackaboodle the SPACE GOD!
HAA HAA HEEOO HOOAA!
Help me, BOSS!

Quackaboodle the Space God has been stuck in this golden hole for a THOUSAND YEARS!
Hee hyee hoople har hyuk!
Help! He's CRAZY!

Now Quackaboodle will use this JETPACK to ESCAPE!
I'm not a jet pack, I'm just UPSIDE DOWN!
Hyee hyee hyee hyee WOOPWOOP!
Oh, we shall see about *that*.

Ha hyee hortle chortle hyick!
Get hims, BRONKS!
BRONK!

Fire fire FIRE!

Wahahahoogle hee ha hyaRG!

Super Backpack, NO!

Boss! I can't help it!

ZOT

ZORP

ZAP

Fire! Fire!
I'm SORRY! Aaah!
Ha ha HOOOP hyuckle hyookle hy yaaaaARGO!
Zap Zap Zap
I'm FLYING! I'm FREE!

ZORP
Nooo.
CATCH

Stop him, BOSS! You GOTTA Stop him.
Fire! Fire! Whee!
Zap
I don't LIKE it!
Zap Zap
Zap

BRONK!
Throw the ARM at him!
It's too HEAVY!
Throws it!
Okay! Okay!
THROW!

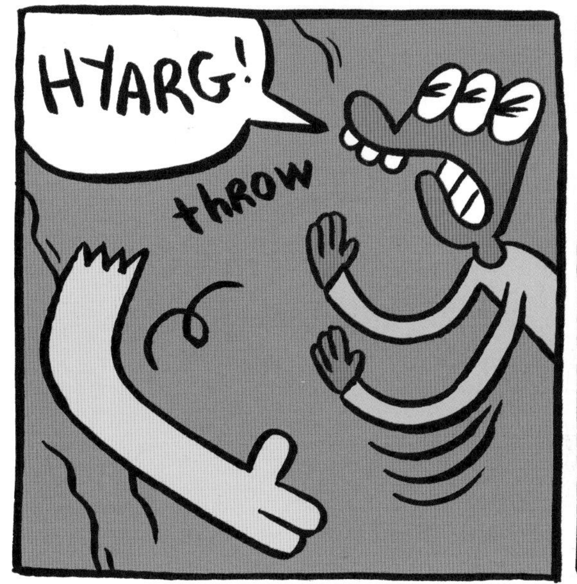
HYARG!
throw

CLUNK

Doonkies help!

BOP

Hey! Doonkies Really DID help!
flip
Doonkies flipped it UPS!
Oh! Oh!
Flippy-doodle.

WUMP

BOING
My handsome hairdo boinged it up even MORE!

phooo
phoo
Gonk help by BLOWING!
AaaaaNNd,
BRZORK
-KICK!
Wow.

Hee heehee hyucklechuckle HA hoo- ...um...

Uh-oh.

Yes! Yes!

flip flip flip flip flip flip

SMACK
POP!
Quack!
ZZZZZZZZ
Ha ha! We did it, guys! We defeated Quackaboodle the Space God!
We WON!
Come up and see.

CHAPTER ELEVEN

Hi, Super Backpack.
Did you miss me?
Yes, Boss.

Like this?
Yay! Back togethers happily ever afters!
Yeah, Boss! That's perfect.
But what about this guy? Him got the X-eyes.
Him look unhappily ever DEAD.
Don't worry! Quackaboodle is just sleeping.
Shh.
He had a really busy day.
ZZZ

Come on, guys. Let's tiptoe away carefully so we don't wake him up.
BRONK.
Shhh...

You know, kids, I'm really proud of you.
Shushies!
shush.
Shhh!

No, I'm SERIOUS. You were incredible today. I think you guys really will grow up to be Glorkian Warriors someday.

Reallies?
Really.
Even Doonkies?
Wows.
Well, gee whiz! Of course you kids will grow up to be real Glorkian Warriors someday.
Because kids RULE! Grown-ups DROOL!
Am I Right?
Am I Right?
Or did I say that backwards?

I mean grown-ups are COOL, kids pee in the POOL!
Don't be so loud, Boss.
Kids fall off STOOLS! GROWN-UPS use TOOLS to eat GRUEL like a FOOL!!

You might wake up QUACKABOODLE, you know.
I KNOW QUACKABOODLES ARE POODLES and KIDS EAT SPICY NOODLES!
And grown-ups draw DOODLES of ZOODLES!

VUMPF
Hey! Who VUMPFED while I was Rhyming?
Cut it out.
That's disgusting.

ZHUMF
VUMPF
UMF
VUM PUMF
VUMP UMF
It's the spaceship of the GLORKIAN SUPER-GRANDMA!
Whoops.
Hi, Grandma.

CHAPTER TWELVE

UMPH VUMPH

VUH-DUMF

BRONK!

She's here!

Yays!

If the Glorkian SuperGrandma is here that can only mean ONE thing, BOSS!

I'm in BIG trouble?

I always file the Glork Reports on time, Boss. That's not it.

Then what?

WHAT?

Gonk Scared!

Who wants to be one of Grammy's Glorkian Warriors?

Hmmmn?

CHA CHOOMF

VA DOOMF

Tee hee!

Of COURSE you do!

PUH POOMF

SHU SHOOMF

Well... get READY! Here it comes!

Weeheeheehee!

I love this JOB!

VUMF

CHUMF

VVVVVV

Oh!

BRONK tingles!
Something happenings!
I'm getting STRANGE new feelings.

stretch
Hlurk!!

PULL
Glurk!

Flurk!
BOING

Don't you want to go in the GROW LIGHT too, GONK?
Gonk scared!
Gonk scared!

DING DONG DOING

ZZZAP

Doonky! You're a pretty lady!
I know!
I know!

Bronk has MUSCLES!
Ha ha!
You do! You do!
Me too! Me too!

CHAPTER THIRTEEN

What cute little grown-ups you all grew up to be. Congratulations, everybody.

Thanks!

I'm proud of you.

Now what do we do?
Go ON OUR OWN Glork Patrol?
YEAH!

GLORK PATROL, GLORK PATROL!
Off we go ON GLORK PATROL!
Ha ha! What a HAPPY DAY!
Bye-bye, grown-ups. Good luck!

CHUMF
CHUMF
CHUMF
Grandma...

Uh-oh, Boss. I think Gonk is sad.
Sniffle

Gonk am still LITTLE.

Gonk was too SCARED to go in scary LIGHT.

Me SORRY.
That's okay, Gonk. Don't WORRY.

You don't have to grow up until you're READY. Okay?

Okay!

Um... okay. Now Gonk am Ready.
Hmm?

What?
Me changed my mind. Gonk AM Ready to grow up NOW.
Really Really!

Really Really?
Really REALLY Really.

I don't know if you'll be able to catch up to the Glorkian SuperGrandma. She's FAST.
Me want to TRY!

Then hurry, Gonk. HURRY!

Wait. Grandma! Here me come!

Here comes your little big GONK!

Well, he's SURE, Boss. AREN'T you PROUD of him?
Yeah.
PROUDLY wowdly diddly doo!

But NOW the top of my head might get cold.
A little bit.

CHAPTER FOURTEEN

GRANDMA!

It am ME!

Here am GONK!

Oh, hi Wendy.

Are you looking for Grandma too?

SNATCH!
Wendy?

Guess again!
Quackynoodles!

Time to WAKE UP and DESTROY the WORLD!
SSSip
Whee hee hyURK!

Hey. This thing is empty.
GRANDMA! HELP! HELP!

Dumb-dumb coffee.
Wendy!

boNK
tumble
doNK

Hey! You just threw Gonk's BABY SISTER!
Oh, so what?

Oh, so what?
Oh, so WHAT?
GONK show YOU "Oh, SO WHAT!"

Really? Is this kindergarten show-and-tell now?
Ow!
BOOT
Wha ha ha heee!

Come on, Wendy. Let's show-and-tell him not to pick on little kids!
Quackaboodle is a SPACE GOD!
He can pick on ANYONE he wants!
Hee hee!

Because QUACKABOODLES RULE! Kids suck DROOL from SLIMEY POOLS!

BLARGO!

Blargo?
Really, how interesting. ...NOT!
BUMP

Gonk NEVER give up!
?

YOW!
CHOMP!

Ow! Ow! Ow! Let go!
Let GO!

WHAM
LET GO!
Let GO!

Let

GO!

Grandma's Back!

Who's Ready to GROW UP!

Tee hee!

chumf chumf

SHINE!

No! No! No!

CHAPTER FIFTEEN

SIGH.
The top of my head is probably doomed to be SAD and LONELY forever.
That's nice, Boss.
I wonder what GONK will look like when he gets big.

I don't think so, Boss. That would be kind of stupid, actually.
Stupid is GOOD.
Come ON!

Oh! There he is!
And Quackaboodle too!
Whee hee hee!
VVV
Hello!
Me feel WEIRD!
Stop freaking out!

This
am

So

CRAZY!
Seriously! Cut it out!

FWASH!

Oh! Oh! Oh my!
What, Boss? What?

Little Gonk grew UP.
Yay!

Look, everbody! Now I have a mustache!
It's true Gonk! You really really DO!
Nooooo! Mustaches are a Quackaboodle's ONE weakness! Oh, I SURRENDER!
Game over.

CHAPTER SIXTEEN

Now go back in your hole and STAY there for another thousand YEARS!

Okay! Yes! Just keep that awful MUSTACHE away from me.

QUAAAAACK!

Bye-bye.

That sure is some mustache you got.
Heh heh.
I know! I know!
And you sure got BIG.
I KNOW!

It's weird, yet also strangely familiar.
Like something from a dream.
It also tickles!
Ha ha!

But don't WORRY, Glorkian Warrior.

Even though I'm big now and have a DREAMY MUSTACHE...
I'll always be your little Gonk.

Wait... REALLY?!

That is AWESOME news!!!
Boss? What are you thinking?

SOON
Now my head will NEVER be cold and lonely!
Yay!
And neither will my NOSE!
Thanks, Wendy!
The END!

EPILOGUE

The end?

RAR!!

Maybe I spoke too soon.

Come on. Don't you remember the GIANT BABY ALIEN that I rescued and NURSED back to health with my own brains?

RAR!

I do! I remember! And here she COMES!

RARR!!
And now she's got an AWESOME mustache too!
Wow!
Baby alien! Baby alien! Remember me?
Remember Glorkian Warrior?
Wow, indeed!

RAR!

She does!
She DOES Remember me!

RAR!
woosh

RAR!!
And there she goes... careening off into space again.
Bye-bye, baby alien!
Wow.
I miss her already.

Super Backpack! I think that was a SIGN. Don't you agree?

A Sign of what, Boss?
That WE should grow mustaches too, of COURSE!

Yeah!
Do it! Do it!
GROW BIG BIG MUSTACHES!

But I'm a backpack and-
BIG BIG MUSTACHES!

But backpacks can't-
BIG BIG MUSTACHES!

Okay. Fine.
I guess it's just my destiny.

Of course it's your DESTINY. We're ALL going to grow the best mustaches EVER!

Actually, I already did.

What FUN!

The end!
The end!
The END!

Thank-yous and apologies

It was such a joy to write and draw *Glorkian Warrior.* Thank you to everyone who helped.

Thank you to my boys, Eli and Oliver. These books were written for you, as bedtime stories. But you know that, because you lived it. And thanks for riding on my back and shoulders. I will carry you as long as I am physically able. You make life awesome.

Thank you to my lovely wife, Amy, for loving me. Without your love I would only be half the man I am and probably only draw half as many books.

Thanks to everyone at First Second. Thanks to Mark Siegel for bringing the book home for his kids to read when I initially submitted it. And thanks to Mark Siegel's kids for loving it so much that Mark simply had to agree to publish it. Thanks to Calista Brill for her brilliant editing of the first two books, and thanks to Robyn Chapman for her help on the third. When Calista said it was perfect already, you helped me find some more ways to improve it. Thanks to Gina Gagliano for setting up so many great interviews and for setting up my book-signing tour, and more particularly for putting me on the wrong subway in the middle of the night in New York City that came to an early dead end. You helped me conquer my fears of the unknown. And thank you to Colleen Venable for doing stuff that I'm not completely sure what it all is, but you made the first two books look good, so I'm happy. Thanks to Danielle Ceccolini for helping me pick the colors to the cover of this book when my first set of colors freaked everyone out. Is it okay that I'm kind of teasing people in my thank-yous? I apologize to everyone I'm thanking.

Thank you to Chris Staros at Top Shelf, for supporting my dalliance with another publisher.

Thank you to Brandon Boyer, who believed in me and championed my idea for a Glorkian Warrior video game very early on. Way before anyone. Thank you Peter Swimm for inviting me to perform at your chiptunes showcase at The Tank in New York City, where I met Mark DeNardo who in turn hooked me up with PixelJam. And thank you to everyone at PixelJam who worked hard on the game and helped the dream come true. Thanks to Miles Tillman for the coding and sweat and the brilliant idea for how to handle the enemy flight patterns. Thanks to Rich Grillotti for your endless geyser of creative ideas. Sorry we couldn't implement them all! Thanks to Andy Baio at Kickstarter for championing us. And thanks to all our Kickstarter backers...you were so incredibly patient. Sorry it took so long to make the game!

Thanks to Mark DeNardo for his awesome soundtrack to the Glorkian Warrior video game. I actually listened to that non-stop while drawing this book. It's the perfect music to draw Glorkian Warrior comics to.

Thank you so much to all the comic book shops and bookstores and librarians who helped get the book out there and into the hands of readers. Thank you so much to the readers, young and old, for joining me on this wild ride. I love your Glorkian Warrior fan art!

And finally, thank you to all the people who I neglected to thank. You're actually the most important of all and I'll never forget you.

—James Kochalka

KISSY LIPS

GLORKIAN WARRIOR BONUS COMIC

AND NOW PRESENTING THE VERY FIRST GLORKIAN WARRIOR COMIC, ORIGINALLY DRAWN IN 2007 FOR THE POP GUN ANTHOLOGY:

GLORKIAN WARRIOR™

Blast 'em, Super Back Pack!

BZORP

How's this, Boss?

Good jump, Boss!

Nothin' to it!

It's easy when you're awesome.

FOO!

Uh, Boss? I can only blast straight up, remember? You've got to jump over them.

What!? I can't jump over them! They're stacked too high!

Then... uh-oh!

THE END

THE REAL WENDY

Whee hee hee!
Who wants to grow up Next?
chumf
zumf
dumf
Pumf